THE WOODCHUCK THAT COULD CHUCK

Written by: Sarah Mickulesku

Illustrated by: Käri Cashen

ISBN-13: 978-1496143143
ISBN-10: 1496143140

For Hayley and Evan
-S.M.

"We are the music-makers
and we are the dreamers of dreams."
~Arthur O'Shaughnessy

For Cade
-K.C.

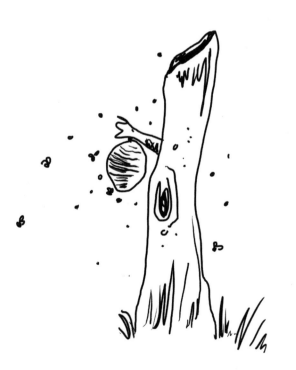

Tell me what is it you plan to do
with your one wild and precious life?"
~Mary Oliver

In a far away village lived a woodchuck that could.
"COULD WHAT!" you ask?

Well, of course, CHUCK WOOD!

He kept to himself in his tiny log cabin
with a few forest friends and an old, rusty wagon.

He told all the folks he chucked wood by the river,
swung a big axe, and shouted out, "TIMBER!!!"

They had all heard of his days in the woods,
and about all the wood that he carved in to goods.

But no one ever saw the things that he made,
just his axe and some gloves that he kept in the shade.

The villagers would gather together and wonder,
"What does he do with all of that lumber?"
He told them he kept it behind a big wall,
but the truth is, he didn't chuck wood at all!

The woodchuck had a secret; it was so hard to keep:
he was too scared to chuck, so he herded sheep!

A sheep-herding woodchuck?? Now there's a thought!
He thought he could fake it and never get caught.

Dreams of chuckin' took up all of his thoughts;
They were there to stay if he liked it or not.

But he just wasn't ready to try it quite yet;
The thought of chuckin' made him tremble and sweat!

He would lie in his bed and picture a day
when his wood-chucking dreams would pave the way.
He imagined a life filled with woodchips and dust;
he just HAD to chuck wood, he MUST! He MUST!

His dreams of chuckin' only grew stronger,
and he just couldn't fight the urge any longer.
On a cool summer day he was fishin' and thinkin';
if he waited much longer his dreams would start shrinkin'.

He leaned over the water and saw his reflection,
stared hard at his face and asked out a question.
He asked this question and he asked it GOOD...

HOW MUCH COULD A WO

COULD

CHUCK IF

a woo

COULD

CHUCK

WOOD

ODCHUCK

dchuck

WOOD?!

WELL...

as much as he believes he can!
Don't YOU think he could?

OF COURSE he could! It's a pretty safe bet
the woodchuck CAN chuck, he just doesn't know yet!
If the woodchuck just believed, he'd certainly see
that he can do anything, just like you and me!

He could skydive from airplanes and land on his feet,

with some goggles,
a harness,
and one bed sheet.

He could build his own igloo,
or teach art classes;
swim the whole ocean
wearing glittery glasses!

He could race on an ostrich while wearing a tie;

walk on a tightrope, closing one eye!

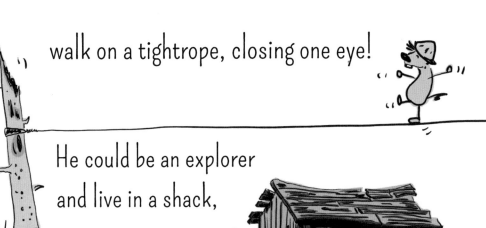

He could be an explorer
and live in a shack,

or ride his blue unicorn
to Africa and back!

He could make an invention
to test out in space
if he's honest, and humble,
and always has grace.

Well, he DOES have grace! He is loyal and brave!
Just think of all that wood if a chucking he gave!

He wondered how hard it would be if he tried,
just took a chance, and no longer hide.

The woodchuck THINKS he can chuck, still, he doubts.

What if he doesn't chuck the proper amount?
Which way is he supposed to swing the axe?

or stand with his feet while he gives it a WHACK?

Well, who's to say how to stand
or how much is enough?
After all, WHO'S IN CHARGE
of this wood-chucking stuff!?

He could chuck wood one-handed while wearing a sack,

or with both arms crossed behind his back!

He could chuck wood in a bright purple coat,
and carve it in to elephant houses that float!

If only the woodchuck would give it a shot,
then he'll never know if it's the right way or not!

He decided to take an adventure to think,
hiked to a cliff and stood on the brink,
    soaked in the beauty of nature and then,
    climbed some more and hiked again!

OF COURSE I COULD!

While he was alone, it all became clear:
the only thing blocking his dream was FEAR!

He stepped to the edge of the mountain and stood,
and shouted out loud, "OF COURSE I could!!"

A trip to the mountains was all that he needed
to follow his dream until he succeeded.

He returned to his village and tried it one night.
He chucked and he chucked with all of his might!

Woodchips went flying
as he whistled a song,

he chucked and he whistled
all night long!

The pile grew as high
as the tops of the trees;
he looked up when he finished
and hardly believed.

In the light of the silvery moon he stood,
just his axe, his gloves, and his love for wood.

He knew that he liked it so he just kept going,
and the woodchuck showed no signs of slowing.

Word spread so fast of his strength and his grit;
with one swing of his axe, a whole log he could split!
He became known for his skill and his speed.
He could chuck wood, all right. Oh yes, indeed.
He looked in amazement at all he could do
and the villagers all started trying it, too!

He had waited so long to do it, but why?
All he needed to do was try!

If he had tried sooner then he would have seen
that sheep-herding woodchucks are just not meant to be.

Once he was honest about who he was,
he felt like flying! Like a kite! Or a dove!

Before the woodchuck realized what he started,
he turned to see that the whole town had darted!

They all started dreaming up dreams so big,
all thanks to the woodchuck and his wood-chucking gig.

The thirst for adventure started spreading, too,
and the village of dreamers just grew and grew!

He inspired the world to dream big and be brave,
all because of a chucking he gave.

Sometimes it takes courage to take a big leap,
then all of those secrets you dont have to keep,

When you dream dreams that are bigger than you,
there is just no telling what things you can do!

Only you know the dreams in your head,
believe in yourself and what lies ahead!

No one outside of yourself, does it seem,
can define or limit the life that you dream.

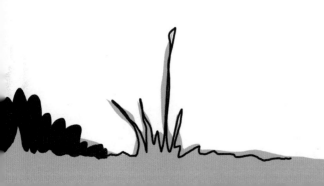

AUTHORS NOTE

I grew up in the beautiful San Juan Mountains of Southwestern Colorado where at the age of seven, I wrote a story in crayon on some sheets of lined notebook paper held together with yarn about a woodchuck who set out to chuck as much wood as possible (which, at the time, was drawn as an actual plaid-clad man with an axe because I didn't know woodchucks were animals, I thought they were lumberjacks). I loved to write and expressed my love of nature through poetry and stories.

Later, I earned my BA in journalism hoping to pursue a career in writing, but never felt compelled to regurgitate the news, I always wanted to write original content. I wrote features for the music section of my college paper and got to interview bands and go to shows for free, not a bad gig but after graduating and starting a family, it was no longer realistic. Despite all of that, my desire to write has never left me.

After my children entered the picture, I felt compelled to revisit the story I had started all those years ago as a child sitting in front of my wood-burning stove in my PJs and pink sponge rollers. I feel strongly that words carry a lot of weight and that kids need to be hearing positive messages during their most formative years that may end up serving them in a beneficial way later in life. To this day I can still remember my first grade teacher reading Aesop's Fables to our class and those messages still resonate with me all these years later.

The story of the woodchuck essentially is a culmination of my love of nature combined with my own unwillingness to concede to whatever standards society has deemed as the "right way" to go about living life. As a child I watched my parents uphold a DIY ethic, always working for themselves and never really adhering to what society viewed as the proper road to follow, and this project was no different for me. I chose to self-publish in a stick-it-to-the-man sort of fashion, just like the woodchuck would do. This story was born out of my deep desire to inspire others and my intense love of exploring and being inspired by the great outdoors. My hope is that through the woodchuck's internal struggle with value and self-confidence, a lightbulb will go on in the hearts and minds of children everywhere who may be questioning their self-worth, struggling to find their path, or doubting their ability to be a leader, and help them tap in to their reservoir of awesome and, in turn, motivate those around them to unleash their awesome upon the world, too. You never know who is watching, who is listening, who needs that example, who appreciates your struggle, or who's fire needs igniting.

In loving memory of my grandpa, Kenneth Warner, who not only proudly served our country as a sailor in the United States Navy during WWII, but served as a positive light and source of inspiration for me. He gave me the invaluable gifts of perseverance, thick skin, determination, and self-worth. He invested in my strengths and cultivated my passion for writing at an early age, letting me take over his lawnmower-sized Macintosh computer and tap, tap, tap away on the keys during my summer vacations. Thank you grandpa, for understanding me and believing in me, you are dearly missed. ("LOOK THAT UP IN YOUR FUNK AND WAGNALLS!") And to my grandma, Evelyn Warner, for always looking up words in the dictionary with me when I was little and instilling in me not only a love for books but a love for the words inside of them.

Kenneth Warner, 1927-2007

Thank you to everyone who influenced my story, and the story of the woodchuck. My high school psych teacher, Abraham Eisenstein, for showing me that it's not what you know, it's how you come to know it. My college design teacher, Liz Bilotta, for stoking my creative juices and giving me the gift of technology as another medium with which to create. My husband, Randy, for pushing me to move forward with writing for a younger audience and supporting all of my ventures, big or small. And to the following friends who served as my sounding board and enormous sources of support during the creative process: Erin Walker, my unofficial editor and grammar chief, Ryan Britton, my business strategist and advisor, Mandy Allender, my head cheerleader and one-woman pep rally commitee, Laney Kolker, for pushing me over the edge of a cliff in to the mysterious world of self-publication, Miranda Ament for teaching me about all things font-related, and to everyone else who read my roughest drafts and believed in me even then. Thank you.

Made in the USA
San Bernardino, CA
10 June 2014